*Before
the
Wildflowers
Bloom*

BOULDER

★ DENVER

COLORADO SPRINGS

PUEBLO

THE MINE COUNTRY
COLORADO 1916

WALSENBURG

AGUILAR

DELAGUA
HASTINGS

LUDLOW

TRINIDAD

Before the Wildflowers Bloom

A NOVEL

by *Tatyana Bylinsky*

Crown Publishers, Inc.
New York

Library of Congress Cataloging-in-Publication Data

Bylinsky, Tatyana. Where the wildflowers bloom / by
Tatyana Bylinsky. Summary: Set in the coal-mining town
of Hastings, Colorado, Carm and her family learn to cope
after the death of Papa in a tragic accident. [1. Family
life—Fiction. 2. Italian Americans—Fiction. 3. Coal
mines and mining—Fiction. 4. Colorado—
Fiction.] I. Title.
PZ7.B9884Wh 1989   [Fic]—dc19   88-34131

ISBN 0-517-57052-1

10 9 8 7 6 5 4 3 2 1

First Edition

Dedicated to the four sisters—
Carmela, Mary, Violet, Charlotte

THIS IS THE STORY of the year I spent in Hastings, a mining camp in Colorado.

Papa was a coal miner, and he worked for the Victor-American Fuel Company. Our street was lined with houses that looked alike, all built and owned by the company. They owned the mine and most of the town.

Papa wanted to leave the mines. Before we moved to Hastings, he started homesteading some land near Aguilar. Homesteading meant that the United States government gave land to the head of a family after the homestead had been worked for five years.

Mama's father built a little house and farmed the land for us. When Papa saved enough money to buy cattle, we were going to move to the land. He loved to be outdoors.

Mama and Papa were from Italy. There were five children in our family. Frank was the oldest. Mary was a year younger than I. Joe hadn't started school yet. Violet was the youngest. Sometimes Mama still carried Violet in her arms.

Aunt Peppina and Uncle Bruno lived next door. Uncle Sam and Aunt Jenny lived a few houses down. We had lots of cousins to play with. All together we had sixteen cousins on our street.

My whole life changed after that year in Hastings. I was only eight, and the year was 1916.

*Before
the
Wildflowers
Bloom*

Chapter One

The sun got up as early as Mama did. The two buckets she carried were silver-blue, the color of the faded night. Cold metal and her stiff cotton skirt collided as each step led her closer to the center of town. Yellow dust circled each footstep. The taste of coal in the ground seeped into the air.

Hills surrounded Hastings. Patches of scrub climbed sloping earth, and the dry ground was spotted with small trees and cacti. The church and school sat on their own hills. In the distance, heaps of slack hid the works of the mine; smoke-stacks cut into the sky above.

Mama followed a winding path along the creek and over a wooden bridge. She passed by the few stores lining Main Street.

The water pump was far from our house. She filled the two buckets and started back for home.

Mama was strong. Every morning Mary, Violet, Frank, Joe, and I woke to the sound of Mama pouring water into the big tin tub.

The light was bright enough for me to see different colors beneath my closed eyelids. I could hear Aunt Peppina outside, singing in her back yard. Papa was already at work.

Mama cleaned out the coal ashes and lit the black iron stove. She was getting the house ready for morning.

"Carm, you snore," Mary said. My real name was Carmela, but everyone called me Carm.

I pulled the quilt. Mary shouted. Violet woke up and called for Mama. Frank and Joe were awake now, too.

"It's all Carm's fault again!" Mary yelled. "She started it."

Mama yanked all three of us girls out of bed.

"Aunt Peppina and I are going over to help Mrs. Bertolina," Mama said. "Her husband was hurt, and the poor woman needs some rest."

"What happened?" Mary asked.

Mama shook her head. "Never mind, Mary. Today I want you all to stay inside and obey your brother. Carm, help me with breakfast. The rest of you sit still."

Helping Mama set the table was my favorite job. The tablecloth was a blue-and-white check print, each square as big as a half-dollar. At each place I would line up the fork and spoon, sometimes one would touch the blue, sometimes the other would hit the white square.

After we ate, Mama left the room to get dressed up. Mary and I sat with our elbows on the table, heads close together.

"Maybe he got shot," Mary whispered. "Papa always talks about Mr. Bertolina's temper."

"*Who got shot?*" Mary and I didn't see Joe standing behind us.

"I *said*, 'Nice day, if it doesn't get *hot*.' Let's embroider today, Carm," Mary said, ignoring our little brother.

Mama's black leather oxfords tapped lightly on the floor as she walked through the kitchen. She wore a soft blouse and a skirt with a tiny flower print.

Leaning against the doorway, Mama held Violet in her arms. Since Violet was so little, Mama didn't want to leave her at home.

They both looked outside. Mama waved to Aunt Peppina as she walked quickly across the yard toward our house.

Thin and small, Aunt Peppina was always moving. She shook her head whenever she spoke, and her brown curly hair bounced up and down. Her clothing was never quite right; her petticoat was always hanging below her skirt. Her stockings drifted and bunched around her ankles.

Mama leaned over slightly as she spoke to Aunt Peppina. Mama had brown hair, too, but it was a lighter color and wavy. Small wisps of hair fell in front of her eyes. She was always brushing stray hair from her forehead.

"Frank, cousin Lina will be home next door, watching the other little ones," Mama said. "If you have any trouble, just find Lina."

Lina was Aunt Peppina's daughter, the oldest girl in her family.

We stood in the doorway and waved goodbye. Soon I could see only the backs of their heads, the size of tiny rag dolls. Joe climbed on the wooden chair. It was shoved against the wall, wedged underneath the window sill. He knelt on the seat, his chin resting on the top of the chair.

Frank went outside, carrying his harmonica. He stood on the back porch. Grainy flecks of coal dusted the porch and window ledges, inside and out. The warm melody of the harmonica felt like sunshine. Neighborhood voices floated through the open window.

"I'll show you some new embroidery stitches, Mary, and we can finish up this pillowcase and surprise Mama," I said.

Mama had pieced flour sacks together with a straight, tidy seam. She made sheets and pillowcases, and sometimes underslips, from the sacks that flour came in. Mama sewed beautifully and could make anything look new.

The flour cloth was bleached a smooth white and was soft from many washings. I rubbed my cheek against the fabric and held it close to my nose, smelling Mama's spices and the fresh air of outdoors.

A faint blue outline of flowers edged the fabric. Mama had transferred the design from a piece of paper placed between a hot iron and the cloth. The flower stems were already embroidered with green thread.

Mary and I sat on Mama and Papa's bed. Our feet dangled above the floor. We leaned over, and our heads nearly bumped together.

I moistened a piece of thread and held the needle high in the air. The thread seemed too thick for the needle; I couldn't push it through the eye.

The thread unraveled into separate strands. As I trimmed the stray fibers with small scissors, pieces of thread fell on my dress.

A door slammed. Water was thrown from a bucket.

"Must be Lina working," Mary said.

"You thread the needle, Mary. The eye of a camel would be easier to see."

Mary frowned. "You mean a needle in the haystack."

"No, I mean the camel in the Bible."

"You're all mixed up, Carm. Next you'll have the camel marching through the gates of heaven before the rich man goes through the eye of the needle."

"Well, it's all pins and needles," I said.

Mary shrugged her shoulders. "Did Lina tell you what she said to the train engineer? He asked her, 'Where did you get your eyes so blue?' And she said, 'From the sky as I fell through.' " We both laughed.

Lina walked in the front door without knocking. She felt at home in our house, and she was always welcome.

"It's blue eyes!" I said. Mary and I went into the kitchen.

Lina's light-brown hair hung in a single braid; her dress was a faded pink. She was even skinnier than her mother. We teased her and called her "Linabones" because it sounded like "lazybones," even though Lina wasn't lazy.

The back door opened. Frank looked in and said, "Since you're over here, Lina, I'll go to your house."

"He's not allowed to leave," I said to Lina.

"I want to talk to Danny," Frank said. Danny was Lina's brother. He and Frank were both thirteen.

Frank closed the door and ran down the back steps.

"Wait till Mama finds out," Mary said.

"What are you carrying, Lina?"

"I brought a magazine," Lina told us. "Look at the cover!"

"Oooh, she's *so* pretty," Mary said.

"If I had a store-bought dress, I'd be on that cover," I said. "Maybe you'd even see me in the pictures."

"Sitting in the audience," Mary laughed.

We huddled around the kitchen table to look at the magazine.

Mary spoke quietly. "Mr. Bertolina got shot. I bet it happened in the barroom."

"Who told you that?" Lina was surprised. "He can hardly move around. His leg got crushed in the mine."

A small drawing in the corner of an advertisement caught my attention.

"Freckle Magic . . . that's what I need. Hand me Papa's shaving mirror, Mary. You could use a dab, too. . . . I'll let you borrow some." I studied my face carefully.

"Well, you'll have to wait a few years, until you collect more than a few pennies," Lina said.

We turned the page.

"Look, Lina, this woman's hair is so short. You were right. This must be the style now," Mary said.

"Lina, when you saw that lady in Trinidad with her hair bobbed, how did it look?" I asked.

"She looked so smart. You should have seen the heads turn," Lina answered.

We looked at the dresses and the newest hats.

"If only we could order that potion. I want to look good for the feast day next week," I said.

After looking at the magazine many times, we let Lina go home to take care of her brothers and sisters. Mary finally threaded the needle, but by that time, Mama had come home tired.

Mary gave Mama a glass of water. "Where's Frank?" Mama asked. She sneezed three times because she was cold.

Mary spoke to me in a low voice. "I bet Frank doesn't want to come home. Mama's going to yell at him."

"He'll be in more trouble when Papa gets here," I said.

Mary raised her eyebrows and looked at Mama. "I guess Frank got bored. He traded places with Lina so he could visit Danny."

"But he forgot to come home," I said.

Papa came down the road as the sun was setting. The only light left in the sky was on top of the clouds. Walking up to the house, Papa whistled to himself. He shouted goodbye to Uncle Bruno.

He left his boots at the front door.

Mama had the tin tub and a bucket of clean water ready for Papa to wash up. He was dirty as the earth, covered with black dust. His skin was as dark as his hair and mustache. Papa stood in the corner of the kitchen, washing his face and arms first. He dropped his gray shirt to the ground and soaped his chest.

Papa sat down at the table. "Frank isn't home?" he asked.

Mama answered, "He disobeyed me and left the house."

"I'll go look for him," Papa said.

Mary opened the front door and shouted, "Frank, come home right now. . . . Papa's coming to get you!"

Aunt Peppina opened her door to see what was wrong. "Those boys went off together again," she called to Mama. "Danny just got home."

She yanked Danny to the door and asked, "Where's your cousin Frank? I thought he came home with you."

"He's afraid to come back. We didn't want to get in trouble. He might be near Aunt Jenny's house," he said.

"I want to go with Papa and help him find Frank," I said.

"All right, hurry up," Papa said as he lit a lantern.

Aunt Jenny lived halfway up a hill, beyond the school. When we got to her house, Papa didn't knock on the door.

"There's no reason to bother Aunt Jenny. It's late," he said.

So we walked around to the backyard. Papa moved slowly, looking in all the dark spaces. He whispered Frank's name as he leaned over.

"Aunt Jenny will come out with a shotgun if she hears voices and sees two dark figures in her backyard," Papa said.

I stood close to him and grabbed his hand. We walked near the bread oven. I slowed down; the bricks were still warm, and the heat felt good.

"What's this?" Papa said. He pointed to the oven. A shoe was sticking out of the door. Papa pulled it, and there was Frank. Papa and I both laughed.

"How did you fit in there, Frank?" I asked. He smelled of warm bricks and freshly baked bread.

Papa was so glad to find him, he didn't really bawl him out. We all were laughing as we walked home.

Chapter Two

It was one week later, a bright Saturday after-noon in November. The air was warm, and the weather was perfect for the feast day of Saint Charles, patron saint of our church.

While saying prayers and carrying bouquets of paper flowers, a procession of little girls in festive white dresses would march down the street and circle the church.

"After we finish lunch, let's go watch," Mary said.

Mama wasn't home. She had taken Joe and Violet to visit Aunt Peppina.

We heard a tap on the window glass. I ran to look outside. Cousin Rosie stood below the window, looking up. When she saw me, she ran to the door.

She said, "I'm so unhappy."

"Rosie, what's wrong?" Mary and I asked.

"I want to be in the procession, but my mother says I can't because I don't have a veil or a dress," she said.

"I can fix a veil for you," I said.

"And I have an old white dress that's too small for me," Mary said. "I'll go find it."

She ran into Mama and Papa's bedroom. I heard her open the big trunk where Mama kept clothing we didn't wear anymore.

"While Mary looks for the dress, we'll work on the veil," I told Rosie.

The front door had a half-window covered by a lace curtain. I always liked that piece of lace. Sometimes, when no one else was around, I had secretly taken it down. I would throw it across my shoulders and walk around the room in a circle, pretending I was going to a fancy ball.

The curtain looked perfect for Rosie's veil.

"Mary, when you find the dress, bring Mama's sewing box with you," I shouted.

Mary ran back into the kitchen with her hands full.

"Carm, you've got to thread that needle this time! Find a spool with thinner thread, so it doesn't take all day."

I held a long piece of white thread between my fingers.

"Don't forget to knot it," Mary added.

I threaded the needle quickly and wrapped the curtain around Rosie's head.

"Hold this," I said to Mary. As she held the curtain, I pulled the threaded needle through Rosie's hair and through the fine piece of lace. The curtain was sewn to her head.

"It needs something, a little decoration," I said.

"What about the old straw hat? The one Mama ordered for you from the Montgomery Ward catalog. Remember, the one with the lilies of the valley on it," Mary said.

I had forgotten about that hat. It was pretty once, but now it was so old and tattered no one wore it.

"Oh, I know! It's in that box under our bed," I said.

Mary carried the hat into the kitchen.

"These will pull right off." Mary tugged the flowers gently and loosened them from the brim.

We attached the little white flowers to the curtain.

"A crown of lilies!" I said.

"It'll be the most interesting veil in the whole procession," Mary said.

Mary held a mirror so that Rosie could see her new veil. She was so happy. She turned her head, and tried to see herself from every angle.

"I think it is beautiful," said Rosie.

We walked to the church and watched Rosie get in line. She looked so proud.

"That's one thing I never wanted to do," Mary told me. "March around with lots of little girls and carry flowers."

Farther down the block, I saw Rosie's mother, Aunt Jenny. The crowd quickly covered her from view.

"Aunt Jenny's here! She'll be mad if she sees Rosie in the procession."

"I'm sure she won't recognize her with that curtain over her head," Mary said. "Let's walk closer and look at all the dresses."

Both sides of the road were lined with people.

We wove our way through the crowd. The procession started and everyone was quiet.

We were standing near Aunt Jenny, but she hadn't noticed us.

As the procession moved closer, I leaned forward to look for Rosie. I held my breath.

"Look, there she is," Mary whispered quickly.

Rosie walked right by us, her head held up proudly. She was walking near the end of the parade.

I heard Aunt Jenny shout, "What's Rosie wearing? She's in the procession!"

She walked to the front of the crowd and grabbed her daughter.

She pulled the veil, and the thin threads broke. Rosie's hair flew in the air. Aunt Jenny threw the curtain to the ground.

Rosie was crying as Aunt Jenny pulled her home.

The crowd cleared when the parade had finished, and I looked for Mama's curtain. It wasn't anywhere. Someone must have picked it up.

When we got home that afternoon, Mama had a question for us.

"What happened to my curtain?" She looked puzzled.

Mary and I didn't say anything. Then Mary said, "Mama, why don't you ask Aunt Jenny?"

Chapter Three

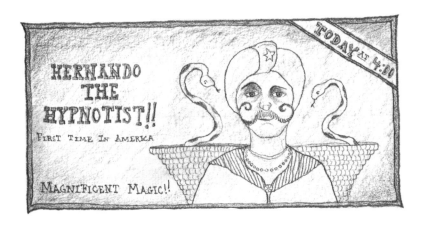

On Monday we were in school. Mrs. McWilliams had her back to the class as she wrote multiplication tables on the blackboard.

A voice whispered, "The hypnotist is setting up his tent on the edge of town . . . it only costs five cents to see a show."

I turned around quickly. Charlotte, one of my cousins, was sitting behind me.

"I heard he'll hypnotize someone right in front of your eyes," I said.

The sound of chalk scratching the blackboard

stopped. I turned again and faced the front of the room.

The schoolhouse had two classrooms and two teachers, a husband and wife. Mrs. McWilliams taught the upper class; my brother Frank and I were in her classroom. Mary was in the other room with the younger students, taught by Mr. McWilliams.

When the last bell rang, Frank said to me, "Let's wait for Mary." We stood outside her classroom door.

As we walked home, Frank said, "There's a show in an hour. I'm going with my friends."

"It sounds scary, people being hypnotized," I said.

"Well, stay home then. You're always scared, Carm," Frank said.

Joe waited for us by the front door. "What happened today?" Joe could hardly wait to start school. He was only four.

Frank waved his hands in the air. "The hypnotist lives in a tent, all year round. He's tall, and he dresses like a magician, with a long black cape. It's lined with a shiny red fabric. He has a mustache twice as long as Papa's, and the ends curl up in big circles. He walks with a cane, even though he doesn't need it. It's just for show."

"Frank, you haven't seen him yet," Mary said.

"Oh, yes, I did, I went to see him during lunchtime," Frank answered.

"Take me to see the hypnotist, Frank!" Joe demanded.

"I'm going with my friends, and I can't be watching you," he said.

Joe looked like he was going to cry. He yelled to Mama, "Frank never is nice to me. Make him take me, Mama."

"It won't hurt you to walk over with your little brother. Why don't you go next door and see if PeeWee would like to go, too," Mama said. "I'm sure Aunt Peppina would be happy if you took him with you."

Frank looked mad. He didn't like to take care of the children, especially when he was with his friends. He left the house without saying anything and soon walked back in with PeeWee.

PeeWee's five pennies jingled in his pocket. Mama had given Joe a nickel, and he held it tight in his hand.

Frank walked ahead and the little boys followed him up the street.

It was dark when Frank returned.

"Where's your brother?" Mama was alarmed.

"The hypnotist asked for volunteers, and Joe

and PeeWee wanted to volunteer. They got a quarter each . . . so they're on their way to Trinidad, to work with him as apprentices."

Mama froze. She stopped rolling out the pasta dough.

Papa jumped up and pushed his chair away from the table. He grabbed Frank's collar and pulled him to the door.

Mama and Papa started yelling.

Mama threw her hands in the air. She was still holding the rolling pin. She shook it above her head and shouted, "How could you come home without your brother?"

Papa yelled, "You stupid boy! Frank, you're coming with me, right now, to see the sheriff. I'm going to send him after Joe and PeeWee."

As Papa dragged Frank out the door, Mama ran after them. All three rushed down the street.

Mama kept yelling, "Hurry up, hurry up!" Far down the road she turned around and ran back.

Loud voices sounded at the front door. Mama walked in, holding Aunt Peppina by the hand.

My heart was beating fast. Joe was all the way in Trinidad!

"Maybe he'll be hypnotized and he won't remember who we are," Mary said to Mama.

"Joe will be back. Go to sleep now," Mama said.

We sat in bed. Mama and Aunt Peppina were in the kitchen.

"That Frank! How could he leave his brother and my PeeWee? He let them run off with the hypnotist!" Aunt Peppina said. "PeeWee, PeeWee, he doesn't know better, but Frank should have more sense!"

Mama was twisting a cotton dishrag in her hands. Her voice was shaking. "Those stupid boys," Mama said.

Aunt Peppina stood by the window. "Here they come," she said as she opened the door. Uncle Bruno and Papa walked in.

"The sheriff is going with Frank to Trinidad to find those boys. . . . they should be back later tonight," said Uncle Bruno. His voice was deep.

Mary whispered to me. "A quarter isn't worth all the trouble."

Papa, Mama, Aunt Peppina, and Uncle Bruno waited in the kitchen. Just before Papa had to leave for work in the mine, when the sun was still below the horizon, a motorcar pulled in front of the house.

Everyone raced to the door—Mary and I, too,

because we had been awake all night. The sheriff walked toward us with Frank and the two tired little boys.

Mama hugged Joe. Aunt Peppina grabbed PeeWee and spanked him and hugged him and cried at the same time.

Papa took Frank behind the house for a good talking-to.

Chapter Four

Sunday was the only day Papa didn't have to work.

In the evening Mary and I sat with Papa on the back steps. A train click-clacked in the distance. A cloud of steam rose above the treetops.

As we watched the sun set, the pines threw purple shadows. I pushed my knees closer to Papa.

"I feel more alone when it's dark," I told him.

Mary leaned on his shoulder and blinked. "My eyes are open wide, soaking up the stars."

"They're like powdered sugar," I said.

"It seems there's more space at night," Papa said. "The world opens wider."

I shivered.

"A blanket would keep us warmer." Mary brought a white wool blanket from inside, and we spread it across our knees.

Papa's face looked so warm I wanted to touch it. My cold fingers traced an outline of red-brown stubble. His mustache felt smooth. I huddled near Papa.

I said, "You have to wake up in the dark and come home after the sun's gone down."

"I won't work underground forever," Papa said. "We'll be growing our own corn and beans one day. We'll live on the ranch, and we'll have our own cattle."

"But we'll be far away from Lina," I said. "Did you know she has a boyfriend? He's Tony Deluca from Delagua, and I want to go to their wedding."

"I hope Tony isn't going to be a crazy bridegroom like Uncle Bruno was. When Uncle Bruno and Aunt Peppina were newlyweds, Bruno got a job above ground on the tipple so he could watch their house during the day."

"Why, Papa?"

"Uncle Bruno was so jealous. He thought another man would steal Aunt Peppina." Papa paused. "Now Aunt Peppina is so busy taking care of ten children, he doesn't worry."

Mary started humming, and I joined in.

"Let's sing 'Come Back to Sorrento,'" Papa suggested. "It makes me think of orange trees and the warm air of Italy."

Mary and I knew lots of Italian songs. Some evenings we would go to Uncle Sam's house and listen to Caruso on the Victrola.

We started to sing. Papa sang all the low notes and hummed his own melody. Mary and I sang the words.

As the song ended, Papa's eyes were closed. A dog barked far away.

"Let's all sing 'Beautiful Dreamer,'" Papa said.

When we finished singing, Papa stood up. "Come on now, my beautiful dreamers. It's time to go to bed."

Chapter Five

After the last class, Mary and I stood outside the schoolhouse. We wrapped our scarves around our throats and buttoned our coats.

Everyone was in a hurry to get home. There was excitement in the air; I could feel Christmas.

Mary said, "Mama's going to bake Christmas cookies today. I hope she makes the ones with icing on top."

"Let's go right home. She's going to need some help," I said.

The sun was trying to see through an overcast

sky. Children were running, some in circles, some in straight lines, all finding their way home.

Frank pulled on his coat as he left the school. "I'm going to bring home a surprise. Tell Mama I'll be a little late."

He ran down the steps with two of his friends. Their boots hit the stone steps loudly. Wind blew their scarves behind them as they walked.

Blue sky appeared as frigid wind pushed the clouds away. We were wishing for snow.

"It isn't really Christmas unless it snows," Mary said. "But once a year is enough." Mary didn't like cold weather.

From far away the house looked warm. The windows were steamed up.

Joe had cookie crumbs around his mouth. "Mama has been baking all afternoon."

The house smelled of a hot oven and sweet cookie dough. A big plate of cookies sat on top of the red tablecloth that Mama used only at Christmastime.

Standing near the stove, Mama swept up crumbs as we drank warmed milk and ate the fresh cookies.

I went to rest in my room and fell asleep. When I opened my eyes, it was night.

Papa and Mama were talking quietly in the kitchen. Papa looked freshly clean. All the gray dust of the mine had been washed away. His rough hands circled a mug of hot tea.

Frank opened the door, his shoulders touched by moonlight. His face was glowing. He puffed steamy air as he entered the house.

"Papa, come outside and help me," he said.

They both walked back in, holding a silver-tipped spruce.

"Mama, how is it?" he asked.

Both Mama and Papa helped Frank put the tree upright.

"It's so full and tall, it's beautiful," Mama said.

Frank sneezed. He still hadn't taken off his coat.

Mama said, "Frank, come sit down, I'll heat a cup of milk. I saved some cookies for you."

Frank sat down at the table, with his stocking feet on the seat of another chair. He shivered. He had been outside for a long time, looking for the right tree.

Joe stood on his tiptoes and took a cookie off the plate. He ran to his bed and jumped under the covers, chewing on the cookie. Frank went to bed too; he was still cold.

From the very bottom of the closet, Mama pulled out the box of Christmas tree ornaments. "Look through these and see what you'd like to use on the tree this year," Mama said.

There were Christmas postcards with pictures of toys and winter scenes. A string was threaded through two holes punched into each piece of the cardboard. The cards were ready to hang on the green branches.

There were garlands. The red Santa Claus was best of all. He was four inches tall, made of cotton, with a big stomach. Mary and I put him up as high as we could reach.

Finally, we attached the candle holders and all the little candles. They were larger than birthday candles, but not very big.

The house smelled green.

"It smells this good, and we don't even have to be out in the cold," I said.

It was getting late.

I yawned. "I'm tired, Mary."

I yawned so much, Mary started yawning too, and neither of us could stop. "It's time for bed," we both laughed.

We looked at the tree one last time before falling asleep.

When we woke the next morning, Frank was already up, and the Christmas tree was bare. His hands were filled with paper ornaments and candle holders.

"I didn't like the way you two decorated the tree. I brought it home, so I'm going to decorate it the way I want to," Frank said.

I was so mad, I wanted to cry.

Mary said, "Just be quiet, Carm. We'll wait until Frank isn't around, and then we'll decorate it again."

When school was out that day, Mary and I waited at the top of the steps and listened to the bell clang.

Frank left the building, and I watched him walk away with his friends.

Mary and I ran home really fast. The brown earth crackled as our shoes scraped the ground.

A plate of cookies sat on the table, and milk was warming in a saucepan.

"Mama must be next door. Let's start now, while everyone is out," I said.

We threw our coats on the chair by the front window and ran over to the Christmas tree. We pulled off all the ornaments, piling them on the floor.

The tree was empty. Mary circled it, looking for the best place to start. We decorated the tree again; it looked right this time.

When Mama came back, she said, "You had no cookies?"

Then she noticed the tree. "You can't change it anymore. It's Christmas Eve!"

On Christmas morning the tree looked beautiful.

Chapter Six

One morning, a few weeks later, I woke up to the smell of fried sausage and ground red pepper. Papa had made his lunch at night, after we had all fallen asleep. The whole house smelled spicy and warm.

I rolled over and made new hills and valleys with the bedcovers. The quilted landscape looked much cozier than the scene outside. The windows had a thin layer of frost. Triangles of white lined each corner of the windowpanes.

Mama was leaning over a pot on the stove, and

rising steam fluffed loose strands of her hair. She called, "The hot cocoa is almost ready."

I sat up in bed.

It was gray outside, raining and snowing at the same time.

I touched Mary's nose with the tip of my finger. She blinked.

"It's snowing, Mary. . . . Maybe there'll be enough for a snowman, but it looks kind of wet," I said.

Mary frowned and rubbed her eyes.

"Come get your breakfast!" Mama called.

The steaming porridge woke us up. I felt warm inside.

Mama put two dresses and two pairs of black cotton stockings on our bed. After we were dressed, Mama combed our hair. She wrapped the curls around her fingertips, brushing out the tangles.

Mama put a scratchy wool scarf around my neck and helped me pull on my boots. Joe and Violet sat near the window, watching us get ready for school.

We got wet before we even left the house. Cold rain and snow blew inside as Mama opened the door.

Frank started ahead. "I'm cold. You two walk too slow."

"I think Frank is just embarrassed to be seen with us," Mary said.

The school yard was filled with students. Everyone was waiting outside for the bell to ring.

As we lined up, I heard someone whisper, "I saw smoke coming from the mine!"

I turned and saw Rosanne Cameron. She looked scared. Her father was the mine superintendent.

When the bell rang, we filed inside the school.

It seemed as though we had just sat down when Mrs. McWilliams asked us all to be very quiet. "There has been an explosion at the mine. All of you are excused to go home."

Chairs scraped against the wood floor, and everyone ran to get their coats.

We all ran home. Flakes of white dotted my coat and quickly melted; the snow was not sticking to the muddy road.

My cousins ran ahead of me. I couldn't see Mary or Frank anywhere.

Cold air rushed against the back of my throat. Water numbed my feet as I splashed through puddles.

I slid and fell. Caked with mud, I pushed myself up. My black stockings were coated brown.

I felt lost. People were running in every direction. Someone was crying. Cousin Rosie crouched by the side of the road. I couldn't speak; I just ran right by her.

Little Joe was in his chair, propped against the front window. "Mama left to wait at the mine. Violet's in Mama's bed, and she's still sleeping," Joe said.

I wandered through the house, wishing Mama were home. I was scared. The air inside the house seemed as cold and dark as it was outside.

Pressing my hands against my face, I ran to my room. Under the red patched quilt was the best place to be, so I crawled into the bed.

Finally, the front door cracked open. Cold air, swirling with snow, followed Frank into the house.

I sat up. "Where'd you go?"

Frank walked into the bedroom. "I went down to the mine to see what was going on. Mama sent me home as soon as she saw me."

Mary ran in and slammed the door.

"Where have you been?" Frank said.

"I was standing in the corner for talking before class. I was waiting to be allowed to sit down, and suddenly everyone had gone. Mr. McWilliams had gone too. He forgot about me."

Mary sat down on the bed, close to me. "Papa's going to be all right, I'm sure," she said.

I couldn't answer. The air suddenly seemed colder. Goosebumps jumped on my skin, and I pulled the quilt around me.

Quietly, Frank went to check on Violet, who was still sleeping. Mary joined Joe, and both gazed out the window. Peering through the spaces in the falling snow, they tried to spot Mama walking home.

All the mothers were outside the mine, waiting for news. Mama would be there for a long time, standing in the slush and snow.

Mary walked back to bed, where I sat huddled up, holding my knees close to my chest. Mary's eyes glistened. She sniffled.

I couldn't cry. My body felt too empty.

We sat for a long time, listening to the quiet of the snow muffling the world outside.

Chapter Seven

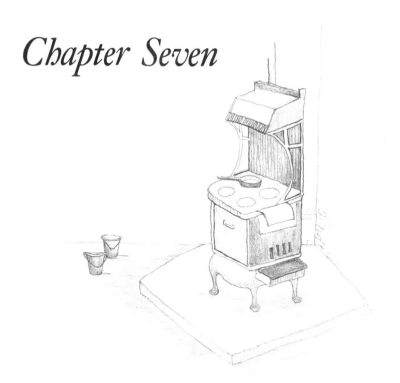

It was noontime. We all were getting hungry. Mama still hadn't returned.

"Carm, why don't you make some lunch for us! You're tall, you can reach the stove," Mary said.

I took the skillet, still greased from the night before, when Papa had fried his lunch.

I didn't know how to cook very well, but the food smelled heavenly. Sliced potatoes sizzled and turned a crisp yellow. I leaned above the warm steam and breathed in, letting it fill my stomach.

Mary and Joe sat at the table. Mary leaned across the blue-and-white tablecloth and talked softly.

"Carm, I'll set the table this time, since you're the cook today," Mary said.

A tiny voice cried out from Mama's bedroom. "Where's Mama?" Violet had woken up.

"Mama's not back yet, so Carm is our cook," Mary said. "I'll let you eat lunch in bed if you don't feel like getting up."

Frank had his head cradled in his arms, resting on the kitchen table. One ear was pressed against the tablecloth.

"Move your head, it's time to eat!" Mary shouted.

Everyone gathered around the stove. Mary held the empty plates.

Suddenly, cold air blew inside. Mama was standing beside us. Melting snow rolled off her wool coat, and she stood in two muddy puddles. Her hands were on her hips, her fists clenched.

"What are you doing, eating at a time like this! Your father is buried under the rocks and you're up here celebrating!"

It must have looked like we were having a party.

Mama grabbed the skillet, holding the hot handle with a cotton rag, and threw it, potatoes and everything, into the snowy backyard.

She stood in the open doorway, just staring outside.

Mary and I peeked around Mama's skirt and watched the steam rise from the snowy ground. The skillet was a dark circle in a blanket of white, like one open eye staring at us. We both started crying.

Mama sat at the table with her hands on her forehead. She didn't speak. She was still wearing her coat and boots.

The door opened quickly. Aunt Peppina walked in. Her rumpled stockings were splashed with mud, and her long coat hung limply. Her hands were red from the cold air.

Aunt Peppina wrapped her arm around Mama's shoulder, and she didn't say anything for a long time. Then she turned to us. "Come over to my house and have lunch with your cousins."

Aunt Peppina put her head close to Mama's shoulder and said quietly, "Go back and wait. I'll watch the little ones. We can't let these children go hungry."

Mama nodded her head and they both walked to the door. I watched Mama walk down the road.

Aunt Peppina carried Violet next door. We all followed her, running through the snow without our coats.

Faces were watching us from behind the windowpanes. Our cousins were there, just as hungry as we were.

Aunt Peppina's house wasn't as tidy as Mama's, but she cooked just as well. Freshly warmed bread never tasted so good.

Chapter Eight

Mama cried in the night. No one else heard her, at least not Violet or Mary, who were asleep right next to me. The sound scared me. I woke up feeling my heart beating and my stomach twisted. Pulling the covers over my head, I tried to make her cries disappear.

Before dawn, Mama jumped out of bed. She was wearing the same cotton stockings and the same dress she wore the day before. Mama hadn't even gotten undressed for bed. She wanted to be ready if they found Papa.

I was the only one awake, so I sat up when Mama walked through our room.

"Your cousins will be home. There's no school. Aunt Peppina and I are going to wait at the mine," Mama said. "I want you to stay inside. We don't know when we'll be home."

Mama left. Outside, a mist of snow drifted above the ground.

Behind me, Mary sat up.

Violet yawned and said, "I just want to sit in bed all day and wait for Mama."

Mary and I wrapped her in the red quilt and propped her head up with three pillows so she could watch everything that was going on.

We didn't know what to wear, so Mary and I put on the same clothes we had worn yesterday. Then we tried to comb each other's hair.

"Carm! That really hurts!" Mary turned around and tried to grab the brush from my hand. I moved to the opposite side of the kitchen table. She wasn't going to catch me. Running around the table a couple of times, I raced to find Frank. Mary and I both bounced on top of the bed, waking up Frank and Joe.

"Mama left already. We all have to stay inside and wait for her to come home," I said.

Joe looked like he was going to start crying and said, "I get the chair by the window."

Frank was quiet.

A fast knock on the door startled us. Danny walked in. His watersoaked feet sloshed on the scrubbed floor. Mama would be angry if she saw the muddy footprints, I thought.

He sat down on Frank's bed.

"Everyone is waiting at the machine shop near the entrance of the mine. The rescue workers just finished their shift, but there's no news yet," Danny said.

Mama and Aunt Peppina were there with all the other women. Mama didn't want us to leave the house, and she sure didn't want any of us down by the machine shop.

Danny whispered into Frank's ear. He jumped out of the bed and pulled on his clothes.

"Mama will be mad if she finds out you left the house," I said.

"She won't find out because no one's going to tell on me, Carm. We're just going for a walk. I don't know when we'll be back."

They both left. I watched the wet footprints until the floor soaked up all the water.

The daylight was gone. Low clouds covered the mountaintops.

Outside, two lights flashed. Frank and Danny stood down the road, both smoking cigarettes.

Mama didn't want Frank to smoke, but he did any time she wasn't around.

As he walked to the house, Frank's feet sank into the thick mud. He stomped his feet outside the front door and started whistling. Shaking the wet snow off his hat and gloves, Frank pushed open the door.

He shouted, "Hey, they're alive! They've found Papa and Uncle Bruno! They're both alive!"

Mary and I grabbed each other and started singing.

I ran into the bedroom and bounced on the bed like it was a trampoline, shouting, "Papa's alive, Papa's alive!"

Mary pulled the tablecloth from the kitchen table. We wrapped it around ourselves and twirled across the room.

Joe ran around us, hooting, and making Indian noises. We pushed the chairs against the wall, then I swung Joe around in a big circle, holding both his hands, until we got dizzy. We fell to the floor, laughing.

Mary swooped above us, wearing the tablecloth as a cape. She was trying to fly. "Papa's alive, and Mama won't cry anymore!"

"He didn't die!" Joe shouted. "Papa's alive!"

Mary kept flying.

Frank was standing by the door with his coat still on. He was strangely quiet.

He said, "It's not true. . . . They haven't found anybody yet—anybody who is still alive."

The tablecloth crumpled at Mary's feet.

Joe walked around in a big circle, then sat down by the window. He tried to find Mama in the blackness outside. I could see the reflection of his face in the glass. He was crying. His warm breath steamed the lower corner of the window.

Violet woke up, crying for Mama.

Chapter Nine

The snow had stopped for the first time since the explosion. Wind brushed my face with the smell of earth soaked with wet snow. The backyard was slushy, and the day was so warm I felt I didn't need to wear a coat.

I was up before anyone else. I was so excited. Today was my birthday. I was nine years old . . . but of course no one wanted to celebrate a birthday. No one even remembered.

Mama left early. When she passed Aunt Peppina's house, a thin figure darted out and joined her.

I could hear Aunt Peppina's clear voice through the closed door. Mama turned her head and smiled; she hadn't smiled in days.

The house was filled with the sounds of night-time—everyone else was still asleep, breathing evenly. I could almost hear them dreaming. I tiptoed through the house.

I said to myself, "I'm going to make a birthday cake."

In my skirt, bunched up like an apron, I put three white eggs. The door closed with a creaking noise, and I was in the backyard. I carried a small tin bucket half filled with water.

Melting snow sat in muddy puddles. Spots of black, stray pieces of coal, mixed with the ocher ground.

I knelt over the driest patch of ground and set the three eggs in a row. A couple of sticks were my mixing tools. I stirred the eggs with a tiny bit of dirt and not too much water, since the soil was so damp.

The mound of earth and eggs was shaped like a rounded stone. I sprinkled drops of water on top to smooth the surface. Along the edge of the oval cake I placed sparkling pieces of rock. Then I peeled the bark from a thin stick and put it in the center of the oval. My cake was done.

I hummed "Happy Birthday" to myself and closed my eyes.

Chapter Ten

Mama came home early one afternoon. In her hand she held a shoe, one black leather boot.

"That's Papa's," I whispered.

"They've found your father," Mama said. She dropped his shoe on the kitchen floor and ran to her bed. Her crying was muffled by her pillow.

We had waited nine days.

I stared at his shoe until darkness entered the house. The shoe became a dark hole against the wall, then it was no longer there.

The room was black.

In the morning, Frank walked by my bed wearing his good suit. When he saw my open eyes, he stopped to whisper to me.

"Mama is taking me to Papa's funeral. Everyone else has to stay home," he said.

Mary propped herself up on her elbows and asked, "We aren't allowed to go?"

"Mama and Aunt Peppina decided the little ones are to stay home. I'm the oldest, so I get to go."

Mary was quiet, but she suddenly looked wide awake. We both sat up; Violet was still asleep, curled on her side, breathing softly. Frank walked away.

"Well, I want to go to Papa's funeral, and I'm sure you do, too, Carm. Somehow we're going to get there. Let's wait until they leave, then plan what to do," Mary said.

Mama brushed by our bed, not noticing we were awake. She was wearing her black dress and dark stockings. She clutched a pair of gloves and her hat.

She turned, sensing two pairs of eyes staring at her back. Her skin looked puffy, and her cheeks were flushed.

She said, "The train leaves for the church in

Trinidad very soon. . . . we'll be back after dark."

Mama leaned over and kissed both of us. Frank and Mama closed the door silently as they left the house.

Mary and I jumped out of bed and watched them walk up the half-frozen road.

"Let's run to the train and make them take us," Mary said.

"Ooooh, no . . . Mama will just send us back home. She'll be mad. And what are we going to do with Violet and Joe?"

"They won't even know we left. By the time they wake up, someone from Aunt Peppina's will stop by to watch them," Mary said.

"Mary, I don't think we should!"

"Come on, Carm, there's not much time." She grabbed my dress and stockings and threw them at me. "Get dressed, there's only one train. We'll miss it if you don't hurry."

Both of us had been wearing the same clothes for the last nine days. We were dirty, and we hadn't washed our hair.

Mary grabbed my hand and pulled me out of the house. Running uphill as I tried to catch up to Mary, I slipped in the mud. She had raced ahead of me. My dress and shoes had a fresh coat of dirt.

"Mary, we don't even have our coats!" I felt like crying.

"Hurry up, Carm. We can't miss the train."

I could see Mama as we ran into the train yard. She had seen us, too. She leaned out the window of the train and waved her hands, trying to push us back home.

A conductor stood at the end of the train, stamping his feet and rubbing his hands together to stay warm.

"Let me give you girls a hand. These steps are slippery." He lifted us onto the caboose.

The conductor must have felt sorry for us. He asked, "Are you going alone, all by yourselves?"

"Mama is already inside," Mary said.

"Hurry and find her. The train will be pushing off soon."

We ran through the train to the third car, where Mama and Frank were sitting. Mama heard us and stood up.

"Since you are here, come sit down," she said. "Frank, run home and get their coats. It's too cold to wander around without a coat."

Frank moved quickly. I watched him darting between parked train cars and over crisscrossing steel tracks. Light snow had started falling.

Mama was silent. She looked so tired.

Aunt Peppina and Danny were sitting right behind us. I hadn't seen them when we first walked in. Aunt Peppina had been crying, but I thought she winked at us.

The train was filled with mothers and children. It was a special train for the families of the last five men who were found. My papa and Uncle Bruno were among them.

Frank raced in, carrying our wool coats in his arms. He was breathing hard. As soon as he walked into the car, the train blew its whistle and lurched forward.

We didn't talk to each other during the long trip. People cried softly. The train made its own metallic sounds. A soothing rhythm led us to Trinidad.

Chapter Eleven

The railroad station was on the edge of Trinidad, the largest town in southern Colorado. We stood in a group outside the big wooden depot. Behind us, I could hear the lumber wagon being loaded. The coffins were being carried to the church by a horse and cart.

We walked together in the direction of the steeple. We were all shivering.

"Rosa," a voice called over my shoulder.

Mama turned. Uncle Joe Vetri and his wife had

walked up behind us. Grandpa, Mama's father, was with them.

The mine superintendent's wife, Mrs. Cameron, waited in front of the church doors. She placed a spray of flowers on top of each coffin as it was unloaded from the lumber wagon.

As we walked inside, I could see rows and rows of pews. The altar looked far away and tiny. Marble statues sat in recessed arches.

Incense burned. The noises of people trying to be silent echoed through the church.

The coffins were lined up at the foot of the altar, all identical, plain pine boxes.

The priest spoke from the pulpit on the left side of the church. His voice echoed, and it sounded as though he were mad that these men had died.

Frank stood tall next to Mama.

Uncle Joe Vetri held Mama's arm as he walked us to his motorcar. We drove to the cemetery on the opposite side of town.

The rows of houses ended. The snow was dotted with dark groups of huddled people.

Mounds of overturned earth and gravel were lined up in a row. Gravestones stretched ahead into the distance.

Mama was supported by Frank and Grandpa; Uncle Joe Vetri stood behind Mary and me. Uncle Joe's wife held my hand. Mary and I leaned close together.

When the funeral was over, we squeezed back into Uncle Joe's motorcar and he drove us to the station.

In the waiting room of the depot we sat on the hard wooden benches. My stomach was growling. Someone leaned over and gave each of us a banana. We were so hungry, and it tasted so good.

The train rattled home and stopped in the railroad yard. Ahead of us, parallel bars of steel cut into the ground and merged, leading to the fast disappearing light.

Aunt Peppina and Danny stepped off the train.

Frank held Mama close to him. Mama stumbled. Jagged outlines of coal chutes towered above their two shapes. Hastings was dark.

Mama and Frank walked ahead into the night.

Mary and I held hands.

In silence, Mama led us into the cold house. Frank lit a kerosene lamp. The wallpaper seemed gray. Black shadows filled corners of the kitchen.

Mama cried. She sat at the table with both arms tight against her waist. She lowered her head.

The darkness was smothering. I was afraid to go near her. I watched her back quiver. Mama raised her arms, her hands against her face.

I put my arm around Mama, and I held on to her until it was almost daylight.

Chapter Twelve

Everything was quiet.

Mary said, "The train whistle doesn't blow anymore. There isn't any coal to fill the trains."

"The only sounds left are the sounds of quiet," I said as I kicked a pebble with my foot. We were outside in the front yard. "I miss the sound of Papa in the house."

"No one has a papa now," Mary said.

Our cousins were outside, too. They were in the far corner of the yard, near the street.

"They don't want to talk to us," Mary said.

"They're sad, too, that's all."

PeeWee watched us, then turned around and walked farther away.

"Carm, they're not going to talk to us. They're jealous because we went to the funeral. They had to stay home," Mary said. Her eyes filled with tears.

We both walked inside, crying.

Later that day Mama sent us down to the pump. Together, Mary and I carried a big bucket. The water sloshed as we walked home.

"It doesn't matter," Mary said as she looked at her wet dress. "My dress will be in the tub as soon as we get home."

"This will be the last time we'll be wearing colors," I said.

We were helping Mama dye all our clothing black, even our hair ribbons and all Mama's cotton stockings.

Mama was stringing a clothesline in the backyard.

She called, "Bring the tub to the back of the house. We'll work out here, even though it's cold. I don't want to splash black on the floors inside."

Mama's hands and wrists were stained as she dipped and pushed each piece of clothing under the dark water.

Mary stepped away and said to me, "Her hands look like Papa's hands, when he was covered with coal dust."

When she squeezed the water from the clothes, Mama hung them to drip dry on the line.

We went to bed early.

I heard an engine. I looked out the window and saw Grandpa. He waved, and I shouted to Mama, "Grandpa is sitting in his motorcar, right outside the house!"

Mama said, "I haven't even gotten dressed yet! Close my bedroom door and bring him into the kitchen."

Grandpa carried a cake with thick chocolate icing and put it in the center of the kitchen table.

"I know it's early in the morning for chocolate cake but have some. I'm going to try a piece myself." He cut a big piece and fed me a big forkful. "It's from a bakery in Trinidad," he said.

Joe was already sitting at the table, waiting for Grandpa to fill his plate.

When Mama walked out of her bedroom, she saw all of us at the table. Chocolate covered our mouths. She smiled. "Oh, Papa . . . my children won't starve with their Grandpa around," Mama said.

Grandpa laughed. He had a soft, low voice. "Rosa," he said, putting his hand on Mama's shoulder, "it's time for you all to come to the homestead to live there."

Mary said, "If we can have chocolate cake every morning, we'll be there tomorrow."

"You can come tomorrow, if you're ready," Grandpa said. "I brought some boxes in my car. . . . I'll help you start packing."

Mama sat down. She was crying.

"Rosa," Grandpa said. "The company isn't going to let you stay in this house very long. Why not leave now?"

We packed all day. Grandpa stood in the kitchen and helped us. His hair had threads of gray and white. His hands were big, like Papa's had been.

"Fill the boxes with your clothes," he said. "We'll leave them by the door, stacked and ready to load in the morning."

Grandpa left late in the day. "I'll be back early, with the horses and the big cart."

The next day, at dawn, Frank and Grandpa carried furniture and boxes to the wagon.

"Our whole house fits in a horse cart," Mary said. "All that's left are three rooms, with an echo."

When the wagon was loaded high into the air, Grandpa spread our red quilt on top of the furniture. We all jumped in. Frank and I sat in the very back. I leaned against the quilt and squeezed into a small space, trying to get comfortable. Mary lay down behind us, right on top of the blanket.

Mama held Violet in her lap. Joe climbed up next to Mama, and Grandpa sat next to him. All four squeezed together on the driver's seat of the cart.

We waved to Aunt Peppina and all of our cousins as we drove away. They lined the edge of the road and waved and cried.

The wagon bounced. The road was rutted. We moved slowly, but the furniture and boxes shifted.

Every time the wagon swayed, I grabbed Frank's arm.

He said, "Carm, you're going to fall out of the cart. You'll just bounce right to the ground, and no one will know you fell out. We'll never be able to find you again."

I was afraid, so I said, "I'm going to get out and walk." So I walked and ran alongside the wagon all the way to the homestead.

We grew up on the ranch. We had our own well, and we could grow corn and beans on the land.